OLiVia'S Secret Scribbles

Box Car Racers

Kane Miller

A DIVISION OF EDC PUBLISHING

Thanks to Jessie and Mia Strobel for all their box car know—how!—M.C.

For Maureen Pollard. Thank you for your patience, support and friendship. x—D.M.

First American Edition 2021
Kane Miller, A Division of EDC Publishing

Text copyright © Meredith Costain, 2019
Illustrations copyright © Danielle McDonald, 2019

First published by Scholastic Australia Pty Limited in 2019.
This edition published under license from Scholastic Australia Pty Limited.

For information contact:
Kane Miller, A Division of EDC Publishing
5402 S. 122nd E. Ave, Tulsa, OK 74146
www.kanemiller.com
www.myubam.com

Library of Congress Control Number: 2020949909

Printed and bound in the United States of America

1 2 3 4 5 6 7 8 9 10

ISBN: 978-1-68464-302-8

OLIVIA'S
BiG BOOK of
PRiVate

SECRETS

DO NOT OPEN!

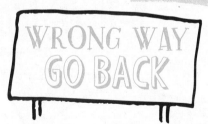

(This means you, Max,
and mainly you, Ella!!!)

Sunday Night

It's Recycling Week at school!

I ♥ Recycling Week. Every year we get to make really cool new things out of old, unwanted stuff.

Like roaring rockets out of toilet paper rolls.

FLAMES

And tinkly wind chimes out of tin cans.

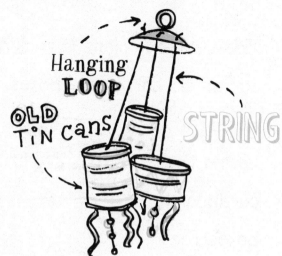

Hanging **LOOP**

OLD TIN CANS

STRING

And ginormous caterpillars out of egg cartons.

PIPE CLEANERS

EGG carton

GOOGLY eyes

This year our class is making new things out of old cardboard boxes. Everyone has been saving their cardboard boxes for weeks!

We've been keeping all the boxes in the storeroom at the back of our classroom. There are so many that they are spilling out the door!

Mr. Platt told us we can work on our project in pairs if we like.

MR. PLatt

Ava and Daisy are working together.
And so are Sage and Samira, and Jamila and Ivy.

You'll NEVER guess who I'm working with on my project.

Hehehe. Just kidding.

Matilda, of course!

Matilda and I have been best friends ever since her family came to live in the house behind ours.

Matilda and I make a great team. I'm REALLY good at thinking up awesome ideas and drawing lots of complicated plans for things.

And Matilda is REALLY good at making them.

I can't wait to get started on our new project tomorrow. I wonder what we'll make this time?

☺livia

LIFE-SIZED GIRAFFE

BIRDHOUSE

DIORAMA

Big Box Monday

Mr. Platt handed out big sheets of paper for us to write and draw our ideas on.

Everyone started talking at the same time about what they were going to make. It sounded just like a room full of monkeys at the zoo!

I scrunched up my eyes and thought and thought and thought about what Matilda and I could make.

Not a robot.
That's too easy.

ROBOT

Not a time machine.
I'm already making one at home.

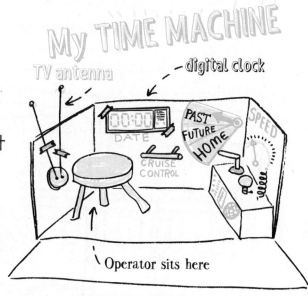

My TIME MACHINE

TV antenna

digital clock

PAST
FUTURE
HOME

SPEED

DATE

CRUISE CONTROL

Operator sits here

Not a castle. I could see lots of kids were already doing those.

I stared out the window at all the different things going on outside.

And then I had a . . . **BRILLIANt IDEA!**

So brilliant everyone else is going to wish they'd thought of it too. I moved closer to Matilda so I could whisper my idea in her ear.

Matilda's eyes grew big. "Awesome!"

Then we leaned forward, curled our arms around our planning page, and started work on our big box project.

☺livia

After dinner

I told everyone at dinner tonight about how BRILLIANT my project is going to be.

Me: Matilda and I are making the best Recycling Week project EVER.

Ella: Are not.

Me: Are too.

Ella: Prove it.

Me: It's going to be a gazillion percent better than yours.

Ella: Is not.

Me: Is too.

Mom: Ella! Olivia! Stop squabbling and eat your dinner. You're making my head spin.

Dad: How about a big sorry to each other?

Ella: Sorry, O-liv-ia.

Me: Sorry, El-la.

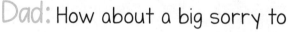

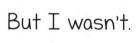

But I wasn't.
Not really.

Big sisters are soooo annoying sometimes!
I stuck my tongue out at Ella when Mom
and Dad weren't looking.

And she stuck her tongue out at me back.
It had lumpy mashed potatoes ALL
OVER IT. YUCK!

Dad: What's your class using
for your project this year, Ella?
Ella: Bottle tops. We've been collecting
them for MONTHS!

Mom: Lovely! And what are you making?

Ella: Zoe and Ammy and I are making a giant mural on the cafeteria wall. In all different colors. It's going to be EXCELLENT.

Me: MY project is going to be HEAPS more excellent than that.

Ella: Oh yeah? What is it?

Me: I can't tell you. It's a SECRET.

Ella: Hmmmmph. I bet it's just a baby thing. For babies.

But it isn't. It's the BEST IDEA EVER.

I CAN'T WAIT until tomorrow so Matilda and I can get started.

☺livia

Project Ideas Tuesday

Everyone began working on their big box projects today. Ava and Daisy are making a puppet theater. They're going to put on a puppet show inside it with their favorite toys.

Curtains

Puppeteers HIDE BEHIND Here

SHOW TIME

Sage and Samira are making a maze for
their little brothers and
sisters to go in. They
need gazillions
of boxes
and rolls
of sticky
tape for it.

MAZE

START HERE

ENTRY

Jamila and Ivy are making a pirate ship!
It has portholes
for spying out of
and a pirate skull
and crossbones
on the flag.

Steering WHEEL

PIRATE FLAG

PORTHOLES

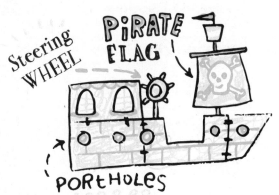

Harry and Nico are making a fierce dragon with a scaly back and snapping teeth.

SCALY BACK

SPIKY TAIL

SNAPPING TEETH

WINGS

Bethany and her friend Mim are making a castle, with turrets and a drawbridge. It even has a moat!

BetHany

MiM

Bethany always has awesome ideas
and designs for projects. And Mim
is really good at building. They are an
EXCELLENT team!

Matilda and I asked Mr. Platt if we could
make our big box project in the storeroom.
We don't want ANYONE to see what we're
making.

But he said no, we couldn't. ☹

So we're making it under our table instead.

With a secret cover to keep everyone out.

☺livia

Painting Fun Wednesday

We spent (mostly) ALL MORNING painting and decorating our big box projects.

Harry and Nico's dragon looks amazing!

And so does
Jamila and
Ivy's pirate
ship.

And Bethany and Mim's castle is awesome. The walls look like they are made out of real stone!

Ava and Daisy and Harry and Nico kept trying to sneak under our table to see what we were making. We had to keep shooing them away!

SHOO! SHOO! SHOO!

Nobody is allowed to see our project until it is 100% finished. Not even Mr. Platt!

☺livia

Big Reveal Thursday

Guess what? Usually we have a big spelling test on Thursday mornings, with really hard words.

But today Mr. Platt said we could finish off our big box projects instead.

YES!

I was just sticking the very last piece onto the back part when he called out, "Time's up!"

Then we had a big show-and-tell. We took our projects up to the front, one by one. Then we told our classmates all about how we'd made them and how they worked.

AVA

Daisy

SHOW TIME

Matilda and I waited until everyone else had had their turn. Then we asked them all to shut their eyes really tight and count backward from 20, so we could do our big reveal!

While they were counting we climbed back under our table . . .

20, 19, 18, 17, 16...

ME

Matilda

stepped into our secret project . . .

15, 14, 03, 12, 11 . . .

adjusted our straps . . .

10, 9, 8, 7, 6 . . .

and stood tall . . .   5, 4, 3, 2 . . .

Matilda called out, "Open your eyes!" just as everyone else was saying, "One!"

"Ta-da!" I said.

Then Matilda and I zoomed off around the room, chasing each other in a big box car race.

It was SUPER FUN!

Everyone wanted to have a turn in our box car racers too. Especially Ava and Daisy and Nico and Harry!

But Mr. Platt said maybe another time. And then he told us to get out our math books because he had gazillions of exciting things to tell us all about numbers.

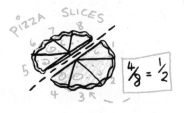

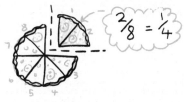

But I couldn't sit still in my seat. I was too happy and excited. Everyone thought our project was AWESOME!

☺livia

Fair Play Friday

Ava and Daisy were waiting at the gate

when Matilda and I arrived at school this morning. And so were Sage and Samira. And Harry and Nico. And most of the kids in our class!

They all wanted a turn in our box car racers! The box cars were still in our classroom, but everyone wanted us to bring them outside.

Wow! It made us feel REALLY SPECIAL!
Just like we were TV stars!

"Maybe at recess," I told them.

"Yes!" said Harry and Nico.

"But only if you're really, REALLY careful
with them," added Matilda.

"Of course," said Ava and Daisy.

"Don't worry, we will be," said Sage and
Samira.

"We're going to be super racing stars," said Milo and Mehmet.

As soon as the bell went for recess, Matilda and I carefully carried our super box car racers out to the playground.
We didn't want them to get squashed or rumpled.

Ava and Daisy rushed forward. "We're going first!" they said. "We're Olivia and Matilda's BEST FRIENDS."

"No, we are," said Sage and Samira, pushing in front.

"That's not fair," said Harry. "Nico and I asked first."

"No, WE did," said Milo and Mehmet.

"STOP IT!" I said. "You are all making my head spin!"

"And you're CRUMPLING OUR CARS!" said Matilda.

"Oops. Sorry," said Ava, stepping back.

"Me too," said Harry.

Then everyone else said sorry too.

"I know," said Matilda. "Let's play a counting game to see who gets to have the first turn."

So we did.

Teeny tiny
Tootsie toes
Catch a sniffler
By his nose!
If he sneezes
Let him go
Teeny tiny
Tootsie toes.
Aaaaa-choo!

And the rhyme
stopped on Harry.
So he and Nico
had the first turn.

They climbed into our box cars and slipped
the straps over their shoulders. But Harry
was too tall. And Nico was too short. Our
box cars didn't fit them very well.

"Ready. Set. Go!" called Matilda.

Harry and Nico raced away across the playground. Everyone cheered them on.

Harry was winning. He went faster, and faster, and faster, until suddenly his straps broke.

NICO

HARRY

And he tripped over.

And Nico crashed into
him.

And our beautiful
box cars got all
twisted and tangled.

And broke into bits.

"Oops," said Harry.

"We didn't mean to crash," said Nico.

Then Harry and Nico helped us pick up all the broken bits.

"Maybe you need to use stronger glue next time," said Harry.

"And thicker cardboard," said Nico.

"And stronger straps," said Harry.

"The race was really fun though," said Nico. "I wish we could do it again."

And then I had ANOTHER one of my brilliant ideas.

"There are still lots of big boxes in our classroom storeroom," I said. "We could all take a box home over the weekend and everyone could make their own big box car racer! Then next week we could have a big box car race challenge at school!"

And guess what?

Everyone thought it
was a brilliant idea
too. We ran inside and
told Mr. Platt. And he loved
my idea! He even printed out
some special box car-making
instructions for us all to use!

How to MAKE
BOX CAR RACERS

I can't wait for Monday to
see what everyone else
makes!

☺livia

Super Saturday

Matilda came over to my place super early so we could get started on our new box cars straightaway.

The first thing we did was find two boxes that were much stronger than our first ones. We didn't want our NEW, IMPROVED box cars to fall to bits again!

Dad took us to the big stores. We asked all the storekeepers if they had any boxes in the size that we needed.

These were PERFECT

When we got home, we took everything we needed for our box cars into the family room. Dad helped us to cut the bottom out of our boxes.

Then he helped us to fold the cardboard back to make our windshields.

Matilda and I measured out eight big sheets of glittery foam we bought at the craft shop. Then we cut them out and stuck them to the sides of our boxes.

Matilda's sheets were sparkly blue. And mine were sparkly red.

They looked amazing!

But then the foam started coming
unstuck again. And the glitter started
falling off. It went flying everywhere!

All over the couch and the floor

and Dad

and Max

and Bob

and Donkey

and us.

And then Mom and Ella arrived back from Ella's gymnastics class.

It went all over them as well.

OOPS!

Mom said Matilda and I had to clean up ALL THE GLITTER by ourselves.

MOM

ELLA

So we did. It took FOREVER. (Although Dad
sneaked back in and helped a bit. And also
Bob. ♥ ☺)

Then Ella came back
in with her Big Box of
Craft Supplies.

She gave us some big rolls of super–sticky white paper and helped us to cut them up. It was really, really hard to get the un–sticky bit off. Lots of the paper got stuck to me instead! ☺

Then we stuck the paper on the sides of our cars where the foam used to be.

We had lots of fun painting special designs all over our box car racers! Like soccer balls. And roller skates. And my favorite animal—pandas!

Ella showed us how to make license plates out of old bits of cardboard . . .

and wheels out of paper plates and
headlights out of paper cups.

Now our box car racers look SUPER
amazing!

☺livia

Test Drive Sunday

Matilda and I took our box car racers to the park this afternoon to try them out.

My whole family came too!

Mom and Dad and Ella and Max played soccer while Matilda and I had a best-of-three race competition.

Here are our results:

RESULTS:

Race ONE winner: Me
Race TWO winner: Matilda
Race THREE winner: DEAD heat!

We were just lining up again
for another race when we saw
someone waving
at us from the
other side
of the park.

Then the someone started running toward us. And guess who it was?

Bethany!

Me: Hi, Bethany!

Matilda: Hiya, B!

Bethany: Hi! Wow. Your new box car racers look AMAZING!

Matilda and me (together): Thank you!

Matilda: We made them yesterday. At Olivia's place.

Me: It took us ALL day.

Matilda: Yeah. It was really fun.

Me: We got glitter ALL over
us.

Matilda: And everything
else! And then all the sticky
paper got stuck to Olivia. It
was SO funny.

Me: We couldn't stop
laughing!

Bethany: That sounds . . . really great.

Bethany looked a bit sad.
Bethany NEVER looks sad.
She's always too busy bouncing
around thinking up new ideas
for things.

Me: What did you do yesterday, Bethany?

Bethany: Oh, you know. Nothing much.

Me: Are you and Mim making box cars for the big race next week?

Bethany: Ummm . . . maybe.

Matilda: I bet your car will be FANTASTIC!

Me: So do I. Just like the castle you and Mim made at school.

Bethany: Maybe. I have to go now. Bye.

And then she ran back over to her family before we could say anything else.
Matilda and I looked at each other.

Something was wrong.

We just didn't know what. ☹

Mom came over. "Come on, Olivia. I want to see how fast you can go!"

So Matilda and I lined up for another race. This time we had a best-of-five competition! And I won three of them!

Mom was timekeeper and judge.

And guess what? Mom told us that when she was at school, her class made box car racers too! And her box car was always the fastest and the best.

And do you know why? It's because it had super-duper silver racing stripes painted on the sides!

SILVER RACING STRIPES

Mom's going to take us shopping tomorrow after school. We're going to buy some special silver paint so we can add our OWN super-duper racing stripes.

Mom says they will make our cars go even faster than they do now! Matilda and I are going to be the winners of our whole class! I can't wait until tomorrow to get the silver paint so we can add our stripes.

But I also can't stop thinking about
Bethany. I wonder why she hasn't made
her own car yet?

☺livia

Change of Plan Monday

Everyone brought their box cars to
school today. Mr. Platt said we could have
ANOTHER show-and-tell so we could
find out all about how they were made.

Ava made an ambulance.

Mr. Platt said this might be useful if anyone crashes into each other again!

AVA

AMBULANCE

AMBULANCE

Daisy made a police car with flashing headlights.

Daisy

POLICE

POLICE CAR

Harry and Nico both made planes. Harry's has a real propeller on the front.

Nico

Harry

REAL PROPELLER

And Milo and Mehmet made a bat car! It has space for TWO racers in it.

Milo
Mehmet
Bat CAR

Bethany sat quietly at her table, watching everyone else showing off their box cars.

Matilda and I went over to her.

Then Bethany told us that she HAD tried to make a box car on Saturday. All by herself. She'd even had lots of brilliant ideas for it!

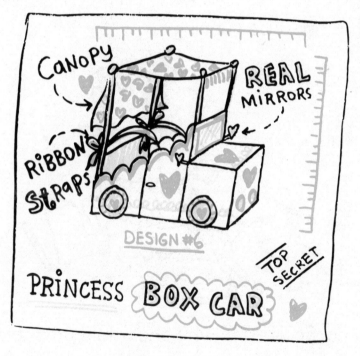

But without Mim there to help her make it, it had looked really wonky.

And when she'd tried it out in the backyard, the wheels fell off. And then the straps came undone. And the car part slipped down her legs and tripped her up while she was running.

Oh no! So THAT'S why she'd told us she'd been too busy to make one. She didn't want us to know it had all gone wrong. ☹

Poor Bethany. I remembered some of Bethany's other excellent ideas that hadn't worked out. Like the time she used a really, really old egg for our bouncy egg science experiment, instead of a nice, fresh new one.

It turned out REALLY stinky. (Pee-yew!)

Or the time
the bottom
fell out of the
bird feeder she
made out of
twigs. So all the
food she put in
there for the
birds to eat fell out too!

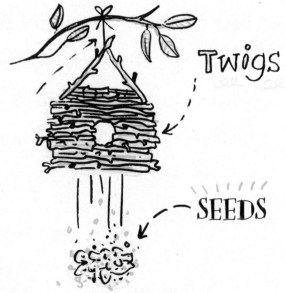

TWIGS

SEEDS

I was just about to say something when
Mr. Platt clapped his hands. Then he told
everyone to pack up their box cars and
take them to the back of the classroom.

Matilda and I had a BIG chat on the way.

But then we decided helping our friend
was the most important thing. So we
went to see Bethany at recess.

Me: Hey, Bethany. What are you doing after school today?

Bethany: Nothing much.

Me: Matilda and I aren't doing anything much either, are we, Matilda?

Matilda: Nope. We're totally un-busy.

Me: So maybe we could come over to your place this afternoon.

Matilda: And help you make your own box car!

Me: And then try it out. We could have a three-car best-of-three race!

Bethany: That would be
AWESOME! Thank you!
I have SOOOO many good
ideas for a new one. I'm just
not sure how to build it.
Me: Matilda is excellent at
building things!

So after school, Matilda and I went over
to Bethany's place, with some extra craft
supplies from Ella's Big Box.

We found a really excellent, strong box in
her back shed. It was much better than
the one she'd brought home from school.

Then we listened carefully to all of Bethany's NEW good ideas.

Bethany LOVES fairy tales. And also unicorns. So we helped her to make a box CARRIAGE racer instead of a car! With EXTRA-strong straps. 🙂

HORSE TAIL

UNICORN head with REAL mane

PINK AND PURPLE DOORS

EXTRA glitter

Bethany's box carriage racer looks AMAZING! And she can run really fast in it!

Here are the results of our three-car best-of-three race:

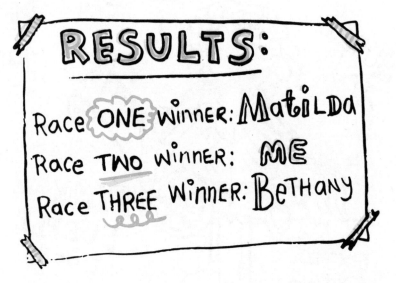

RESULTS:

Race ONE winner: MatiLDa
Race TWO winner: ME
Race THREE winner: BeTHany

I wonder who will win the big box car race at school!

I hope it's one of us!

Olivia

A few minutes later . . .

Oops! I've been so busy today I almost forgot to tell you.

Ella and her BFFs Zoe and Ammy finished their Recycling Week project today. And it's so good, their teacher, Ms. Weiss, put their names forward for a special Recycling Week award.

Here's a picture of it, on the side of our cafeteria at school. There are GAZILLIONS of bottle tops in it, in all different colors. That's *A LOT* of bottles.

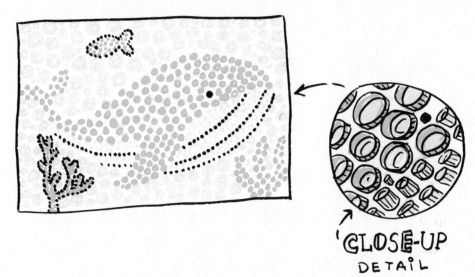

CLOSE-UP
DETAIL

A lady from the local newspaper came
and took their photo, standing next to
their mural.

ELLA   ZOE   Ammy

Ella's mural is pretty good. But our box car racers are SENSATIONAL.

I hope the lady comes back tomorrow when we have our big box car race!

☺livia

Race Day Tuesday

We had our big box car race today!

As soon as the bell went for lunchtime, we all climbed into our cars.

Then we walked together, in a big crocodile line, across to the running track on the school field.

Lots of kids from other classes followed so they could cheer us on while they watched our race!

Our school principal, Mr. Martini, dressed up in a special judge's outfit. He looked really funny. ☺

And two of the teachers, Ms. Weiss and Mr. Zugaro, dressed up like nurses! They stood at the side of the track with a big stapler and rolls of sticky tape. Bethany told us it was so they could patch people's cars up if they fell to bits during the race.

There are too many kids in our class to all run at the same time. So Mr. Platt divided us up into three groups.

Jamila and Ivy were in Heat One, with Harry and Nico.

Bethany was in
Heat Two, with
Sage and Samira,
and Milo and
Mehmet.

And Matilda and
I were in Heat
Three, with Ava and Daisy.

Mr. Platt stood on the side of the track and read out the rules.

RULE ONE: No pushing or bumping into other racers.

RULE TWO: Any bits that fall off during a race must be cleared from the track before the next heat begins.

RULE THREE: You MUST STILL BE WEARING your box car at the end of the race or YOU WILL BE DISQUALIFIED!!!

The kids in the first heat lined up at the starting line.

Mr. Platt held up a checkered flag, just like they do in REAL race car races. He waved it in the air a few times, then pointed it down toward the ground.

"And . . . GO!" he yelled.

Harry and Nico raced to the front of the group in their planes. They were going so

fast it looked like they were really flying!
Then one of Nico's wings fell off. And also
his propeller. He tripped over the propeller
and went out of the race.

NICO-->

WINNER OF HEAT ONE: Harry

Now it was Bethany's group's turn.
Mr. Platt waved his checkered flag around
again. "And . . . GO!" he shouted.

Milo and Mehmet's bat car looked amazing.
But it was so heavy it slowed them down.

Milo and Mehmet climbed out of their
bat car and hurtled toward the finish line
without it.

"YES!" they screamed
as they crossed the line
before everyone else.

"OUT!" called Mr. Martini.
"You've just broken Rule
Number Three!"

All the other racers were still running.
Sage and Samira were fast. And so were
Jamie and Molly. But Bethany was faster.
She won her heat easily.

"YES!" Matilda and I called
out. "GO, BETHANY!"

WINNER OF HEAT TWO:
Bethany

Finally it was time for our heat.

Mr. Platt waved his flag . . .

And we were off! Matilda and I ran as fast as we could. But Ava's ambulance was beating us!

Then one of her wheels fell off. And so did her siren! And her back doors! She stopped running so she could pick them all up. And Matilda and I flew past her.

Then Matilda's foot
kicked a stone in the
middle of the track! She
wibbled and wobbled,
and wobbled and wibbled.
Luckily she didn't fall
over, but her wibbling
and wobbling slowed her down.

I flashed past her for
the win!

WINNER OF HEAT
THREE: Olivia
(me!!!)

It was time for the finals race. I lined up next to Harry and Bethany.

"Go, Olivia!" a voice called from the crowd.

"You can do it!" called another one.

I turned around. It was Ella and her BFFs Zoe and Ammy. I gave them a big wave, and they all gave me the thumbs-up sign.

Mr. Platt was holding up the flag again. I put my head down, ready to start racing.

"And . . . GO!" he called, for the final time.

I ran like the wind, as fast as I could. But so did Harry and Bethany.

Both of them pulled in front of me, at exactly the same time!

"YES!" screamed Matilda, as Bethany raced over the line, just in front of Harry.

I came third. 😞

I felt a bit sad about that. Everyone likes to win.

And maybe if Matilda and I hadn't helped Bethany make her box car, we'd have had

time to add Mom's super-
duper silver racing stripes
to our own cars, to make
them go faster.

And I might have won.

But who knows? Maybe Bethany's unicorn
carriage was always going to be faster
than mine anyway. Even if we'd had the
silver stripes!

Bethany had designed it. And we'd helped
her to make the WINNING CAR!

That felt REALLY good. ☺☺☺

And guess what? The lady from the newspaper DID come to our race. And she asked if she could take Bethany's photo. But Bethany told her that Matilida and I helped to build the winning car. So we should be in the photo too.

So now we're ALL going to be in the local paper next week!

☺livia